THERE'S AN ALLIGATOR UNDER MY BED

written and illustrated by MERCER MAYER

Dial Books for Young Readers / New York

Published by Dial Books for Young Readers
375 Hudson Street
New York, New York 10014

Copyright © 1987 by Mercer Mayer
All rights reserved
Design by Nancy R. Leo
Printed in Hong Kong by South China Printing Company
W
5   7   9   10   8   6

Library of Congress Cataloging in Publication Data

Mayer, Mercer, 1943–
There's an alligator under my bed.

Sequel to: There's a nightmare in my closet.
Summary: The alligator under his bed makes a boy's bedtime
a hazardous operation, until he lures it out of
the house and into the garage.
[1. Alligators—Fiction. 2. Bedtime—Fiction.]
I. Title. II. Title: There is an alligator under my bed.
PZ7.M462The 1987   [E]   86-19944
ISBN 0-8037-0374-0
ISBN 0-8037-0375-9 (lib. bdg.)

*The art for each picture consists of pen, ink, and watercolor washes
which are color-separated and reproduced in full color.*

To Alburn and Phillip

There used to be an alligator under my bed.

When it was time to go to sleep,
I had to be very careful

because I knew he was there.

But whenever I looked,
he hid...or something.

So I'd call Mom and Dad.

But they never saw it.

It was up to me.
I just had to do something
about that alligator.

So I went to the kitchen
to get some alligator bait.

I filled a paper bag full
of things alligators like to eat.

I put a peanut butter sandwich,
some fruit, and the last piece
of pie in the garage.

I put cookies down the hall.

I left fresh vegetables on the stairs.

I put a soda and some candy
next to my bed.
Then I watched and waited.

Sure enough, out he came
to get something to eat.

Then I hid in the hall closet.

I followed him down the stairs.

I followed him down the hall.

When he crawled into the garage,

I slammed the door and locked it.

Then I went to bed.
There wasn't even any mess to clean up.

Now that there is an alligator in the garage,
I wonder if my dad will have any trouble
getting in his car tomorrow morning.

I'll just leave him a note.